April Fools

April Fools

Fernando Krahn

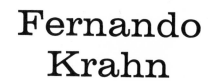

E. P. Dutton & Co., Inc.   New York

Library of Congress Cataloging in Publication Data

Krahn, Fernando.   April fools.
SUMMARY: Two boys create a monster that mysteriously
appears and disappears all over town until they have
to reveal their prank to get out of a tight spot.
[1. April Fools' day—Fiction.
2. Stories without words]   I. Title.
PZ7.K8585Ap   [E]   73-16279   ISBN 0-525-25825-6

Published simultaneously in Canada by Clarke,
Irwin & Company Limited, Toronto and Vancouver

Printed in the U.S.A.   First Edition

To Matias Krahn

FERNANDO KRAHN was born in Santiago, Chile, and studied there before coming to New York City to begin a successful career as a children's book illustrator and cartoonist for national magazines. At present Mr. Krahn, his wife, and their three children live in Barcelona, Spain, where he hopes to devote full time to illustrating children's books.

Mr. Krahn believes that pictures can sometimes be designed to tell a story all by themselves, as captionless cartoons often do. He prepared his art as pen-and-ink drawings, with a separate overlay for the second color. The display type is set in Cooper Black and Fortune Light. The book is printed by offset.